Goodnight

Michaela Morgan
Illustrated by Juanita Downey

Billy sees a monster.

He thinks he sees a monster.

He thinks he sees a monster,
so he s-c-r-e-a-m-s.

Milly puts the light on.

She comes and puts the light on.

"Nothing to be scared of. Goodnight. Sweet dreams!"

Billy sees a dragon.

He thinks he sees a dragon.

He thinks he sees a dragon,
so he **s-c-r-e-a-m-s**.

Milly puts the light on.

She comes and puts the light on.

"Nothing to be scared of. Goodnight. Sweet dreams!"

9

But Billy sees a ghost now.
He thinks he sees a ghost now.
He thinks he sees a ghost now,
so he s-c-r-e-a-m-s.

Milly puts the light on.
She comes and puts the light on.

She pulls back the curtains.

"See, there's nothing there!"

Now Billy's safe and sleepy.

He knows there's nothing creepy.

Goodnight Billy.

Goodnight. Sweet dreams.